FOR MY GIRLS
— S. H. A.

TO THE MEMORY OF PHILEMON STURGES
— W. Z.

Text copyright © 2007 by Sharon Hart Addy
Illustrations copyright © 2007 by Wade Zahares

www.houghtonmifflinbooks.com

The text of this book is set in Clarendon.
The illustrations are pastel.

Library of Congress Cataloging-in-Publication Data

Addy, Sharon.
Lucky Jake / by Sharon Hart Addy ; illustrated by Wade Zahares.
p. cm.
Summary: While panning for gold with his pa, Jake adopts a pig that he names Dog.
ISBN 0-618-47286-X (hardcover)
[1. Gold miners—Fiction. 2. Pigs—Fiction. 3. Pigs as pets—Fiction. 4. Pets—Fiction.] I. Zahares, Wade, ill. II. Title.
PZ7.A257Luc 2006
[Fic]—dc22

2005003917
ISBN-13: 978-0618-47286-4

Printed in China
SCP 10 9 8 7 6 5 4 3 2 1

LUCKY JAKE

SHARON HART ADDY ILLUSTRATED BY WADE ZAHARES

HOUGHTON MIFFLIN COMPANY
BOSTON 2007

Jake stood next to Pa, ankle-deep in the
cold water of Crystal Creek.

While they panned for gold, Jake thought about dogs. He thought about having a dog to play catch with. He thought about having a dog to run with. He wondered if he had enough gold in his pouch to buy a dog.

Then Pa yelled, "Wah-whoo! A gold nugget! A gen-u-ine GOLD nugget!"

Pa whooped and danced in the creek. "We can buy real food!" he hollered. "Eggs, beefsteak, potatoes! No more beans! Come on, Jake! We're going to town!"

Pa took off running.

Jake raced after him.

While Pa piled up supplies, Jake asked the storekeep, "You got any dogs?"

The storekeep said, "Nope. But I got a runty pig."

Jake patted the pig. The pig grunted and rubbed against him. When Jake walked across the store, the pig followed him. Jake asked, "Do pigs make good pets?"

The storekeep said, "Why not? They got four legs, floppy ears, and a tail."

Jake eyed the pig. It did have four legs, floppy ears, and a tail.

Jake named the pig Dog.

On the way home, Dog trotted next to Jake. Pa gave Dog a funny look.

Jake said, "I wanted a dog, but this pig should do. I'm glad the storekeep had him."

Pa grinned and said, "That sure was lucky."

Jake said, "Yup. Lucky."

Between spells of panning for gold, Jake tried to teach Dog tricks. Dog wouldn't chase a stick, but he let Jake pet him, he followed Jake around, and he slept next to Jake's bed.

One chilly night, Jake covered up with Pa's overcoat.

Dog pulled on the coat's sleeve, then sent up a racket of grunting and pawing.

Jake rescued the coat and reached through the hole in Pa's pocket. Deep in the coat's lining, Jake found seed corn from when Pa tried farming.

The next day, Jake scraped three rows in the dirt behind the shack. He built a fence around them to keep Dog out, dropped the corn into the rows, and watered it.

Jake watered the corn every day.

Dog watched and waited.

The corn sprouted.

Stalks grew.

Ears formed.

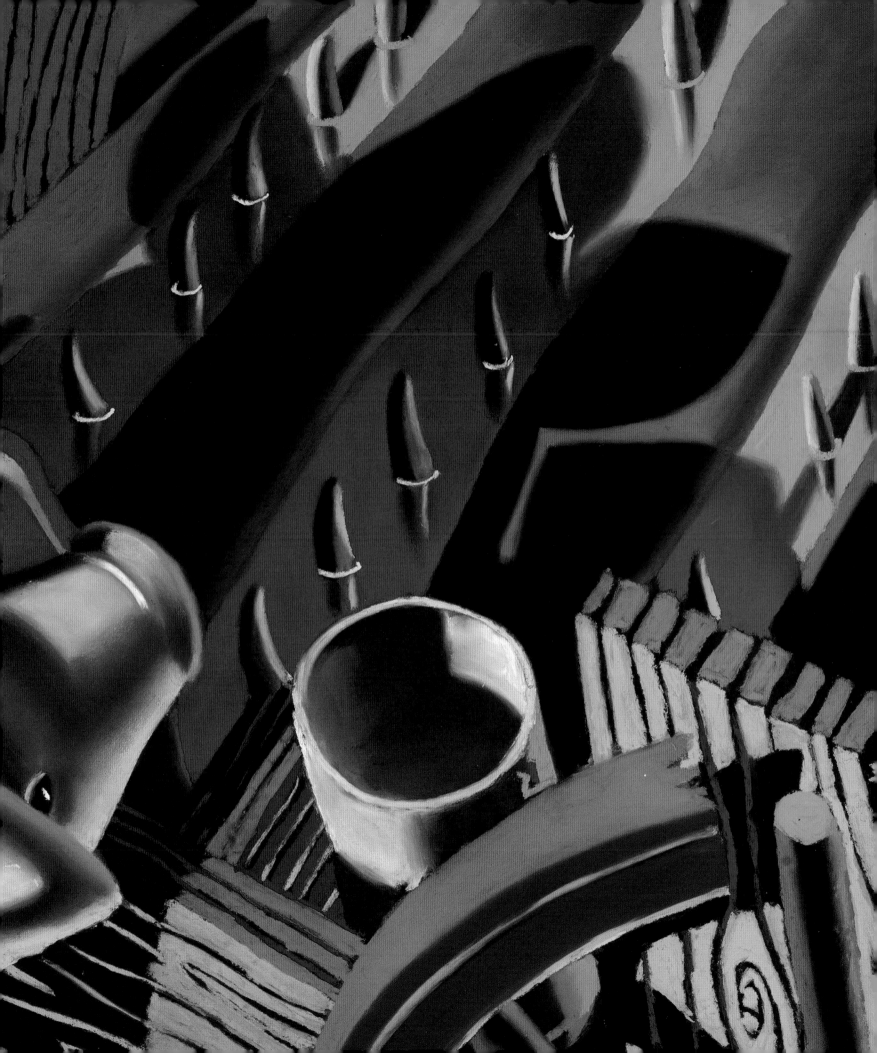

When the corn's silk browned, Pa and Jake boiled a few ears. Dog watched and waited.

After they all stuffed themselves, Pa said, "That was good. I didn't think corn would grow here."

Pa grinned and said, "That was lucky."

Jake said, "Yup. Lucky."

The next morning, Jake went to pick corn for breakfast. Two stalks looked chewed on. Jake sat right down to guard the corn. Dog kept him company.

When dusk fell, a shaggy, four-legged animal stepped from the brush. Dog oinked. The critter ran. Jake threw Pa's coat over the animal's head and held on tight. The critter stopped so fast that Jake flew.

Jake landed on the ground looking up at a nanny goat. Dog oinked and squealed while Jake wrestled the animal to the shack.

Jake shouted, "Pa, I caught the critter eating our corn."

Pa grinned and said, "That sure was lucky."

Jake said, "Yup. Lucky."

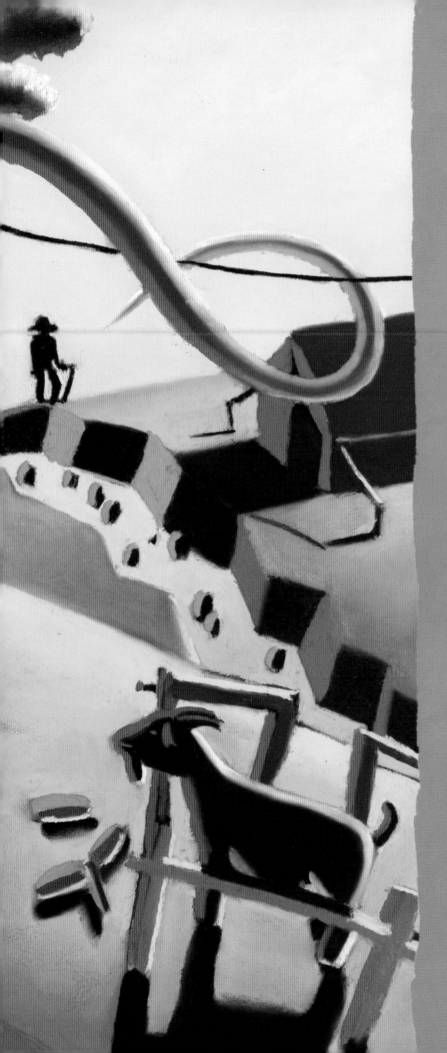

The next morning, Jake and Pa built a pen for Nanny. Jake picked more corn. Pa milked the goat. Dog watched and waited. While Dog and Nanny enjoyed the cobs, Jake and Pa feasted on corn fritters and milk.

The smell of corn fritters drifted down the creek and lured Rusty to their camp. Rusty tucked into a fritter. He licked his fingers and said, "That's the best grub I've had since I left Carolina."

That afternoon, Whiskers
sauntered up the creek. He
patted Dog. Then he stuck
his chin at Jake and said, "I
heard you got milk. I ain't
had milk since last fall. I'll
trade my lantern for a cup."

So, Jake milked Nanny
and took the lantern.

At dusk, Pa lit the lantern.
He grinned and said,
"That sure was lucky."

Jake said, "Yup. Lucky."

At sunrise the next morning, Jake woke to a knock on the door. Jake stepped over Dog and opened the door. A line of prospectors stood outside. Each of them held a plate, a cup, and something to trade. Jake, Pa, and Dog peered at the prospectors. Pa said, "Guess we'll try our hand at restauranteering."

Jake collected the trades while Pa dished out corn fritters.

By noon, a stack of blankets, lanterns, picks, and canteens filled one corner of the shack.

Jake arranged the goods. By sundown, when the line formed again, he was ready for business.

Pa made flapjacks and served them with coffee. Dog sniffed for scraps. Jake took in more trade goods.

Grizzly stepped up to Jake. He glared at Jake and pointed to Nanny. Grizzly said, "That goat is mine."

Jake swallowed hard. He said, "We'll trade a stack of flap-jacks and a cup of coffee for the goat."

Grizzly held out his plate and Pa filled it.

Grizzly frowned and added, "I'm heading for new ground tomorrow. The nanny has a kid. Will you take her, too?"

Jake added two flapjacks to Grizzly's plate.

Grizzly walked away.

Pa grinned and said, "That sure was lucky."

Jake said, "Yup. Lucky."

After that, every day at sunup and sundown prospectors lined up for grub. Pa gave up hunting for gold to concentrate on cooking. Jake handled the store. Dog kept him company.

Before the snow swirled, Jake and Pa built a barn for Nanny and Little Nanny. Then they stuck a lean-to onto the store so they could sleep indoors.

When the creek froze, Jake, Pa, and Dog warmed themselves by the store's potbellied stove.

"Next spring," Pa said, "we'll get back to prospecting. We didn't strike it rich this year, but everything turned out just fine." Pa grinned and said, "That sure was lucky."

Jake said, "Yup. Lucky." He patted Dog.

Then Jake tucked away a pouch of corn
so they could be lucky again next spring.